Five reasons why you'll love Isadora Moon...

Meet the magical,
fang-tastic Isadora Moon!

Isadora's cuddly toy, Pink Rabbit,
has been magicked to life!

It's baby sister
Honeyblossom's
BIG moment!

Isadora helps
look after her mum.

Enchanting
pink and black
pictures!

How would you help someone suffering from the fairy flu feel better?

I'd be their nurse and give them magic medicine made from flower petals. —Aaradhya

I would tell them a funny story to make them laugh. —Sarra

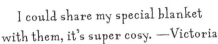

I could share my special blanket with them, it's super cosy. —Victoria

I'd put my pyjamas on and snuggle up
on the sofa with them.
—Nancy

I would draw them a pretty picture with lots
of colourful fairies and give it to them.
—Amina

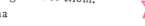

I'd make them a special fairy flu
card with stickers and hearts to
show that I care about them.
—Chia

We could play a game together, like
hide-and-seek, but not too fast so they
don't get out of breath.
—Amber

Family Tree

My Mum
Countess Cordelia
Moon

Baby Honeyblossom

My Dad
Count Bartholomew
Moon

Me!
Isadora Moon

Pink Rabbit

For vampires, fairies, and humans everywhere!

Illustrated by Mike Garton,
based on original artwork by Harriet Muncaster

OXFORD
UNIVERSITY PRESS

Great Clarendon Street, Oxford OX2 6DP
Oxford University Press is a department of the University of Oxford.
It furthers the University's objective of excellence in research, scholarship,
and education by publishing worldwide. Oxford is a registered trade mark
of Oxford University Press in the UK and in certain other countries

British Library Cataloguing in Publication Data

Data available

ISBN: 978-0-19-277810-9

1 3 5 7 9 10 8 6 4 2

Printed in China

The manufacturing process conforms to the
environmental regulations of the country of origin

MIX
Paper | Supporting
responsible forestry
FSC
www.fsc.org
FSC® C020056

ISADORA ★ MOON

Helps Out

Harriet Muncaster

OXFORD
UNIVERSITY PRESS

Ameera-Rose,
Happy Reading!
with love, magic
and sparkle.

Harriet Muncaster

x

Chapter ONE

It was a bright and sparkly spring morning, and I opened my eyes to sunshine streaming through the arched window of my turret bedroom.

'Oh, Pink Rabbit,' I exclaimed. 'It's such a perfect day for a picnic by the stream!'

I leapt out of bed and flew downstairs

1

to the kitchen, flapping my bat-like
vampire-fairy wings. Mum wasn't there
but Dad was standing by the fridge
drinking a glass of red juice and looking
windswept. He must have just arrived
home from his nightly flight. My dad is a
vampire and stays up most nights, soaring
high among the stars.

'Good evening, Isadora,' he said. 'I mean *morning*, sorry!'

'Hi, Dad!' I said, hopping up and down excitedly. 'It looks like it's going to be such a nice day! We could go for a picnic and splash in the stream and make flower crowns and eat peaches and . . .'

Dad glanced out of the window at the sunshine and looked a little worried. 'I'd better get forty winks first if we're going on a picnic . . .'

'Oh, but can't we leave *now*?' I asked. 'You can snooze under your big black parasol!'

'It's only six in the morning, Isadora!' he laughed. 'And besides, we haven't even talked to Mum yet. Where is she, anyway? She's usually the first one up . . .'

'Let's go and ask her!' I cried, grabbing Pink Rabbit's paw and running out of the kitchen. Pink Rabbit used to be my favourite stuffed toy, but my mum magicked him alive for me with her fairy wand!

Dad caught up just as I pushed open the door of his and Mum's bedroom and we both peered inside. The curtains were drawn, tissues littered the floor and there was a sniffling sound coming from the bed. Through the gloom, I could just about see Mum lying there, her pink hair splayed across the pillow.

'Cordelia?' whispered Dad. 'Are you awake? Are you . . . alive?'

Mum lifted herself up on the pillows with a groan.

'I think I've got . . .' she said, pausing to sneeze, 'Atishoo! The *fairy flu*!'

My heart sank down into my fluffy pompom slippers. Fairy flu is the worst! There was no point even *suggesting* we all go out for a picnic! And it would be no fun for Dad, me, and Honeyblossom to go without Mum, knowing she was stuck in bed, feeling poorly.

'What's the matter, Isadora?' asked Mum. 'You look very glum . . .'

'Oh, it's nothing!' I said, pasting a bright smile onto my face, even though inside I felt very disappointed. Mum didn't look very happy either. I guess being sick in bed wasn't her ideal way to spend the day. 'I'm just sorry you're ill.'

'Me too,' said Dad. 'Poor Cordelia!

Can I get you anything to help you feel better?'

'I think I could just about manage some strawberries for breakfast,' said Mum. 'After I've had a little nap.'

'Strawberries?' said Dad. 'Yes! That's a very good idea. Red food is the *best*! I'll go and fetch some from the fridge.'

'Oh no,' said Mum. 'They're in my vegetable patch! You'll need to pick them.'

'Ah,' said Dad trying not to look too dismayed. He glanced out of the window at the bright sunshine and blinked his sensitive vampire eyes. 'No worries! I shall just get my sunglasses and parasol.'

Just then there came a wailing sound

from the room next door.

'Honeyblossom's awake then,' sighed Mum. 'Please would you fetch her, Bartholomew? And her pink milk too?'

'Yes,' said Dad, running his hand through his hair and starting to look a bit flustered. 'OK, yes. I'll get Honeyblossom up and fed, then sunglasses, parasol, strawberries, and—'

'Wait!' I said. 'I can go and pick the strawberries, Dad! I'm happy to make Mum's breakfast! I'll bring it up on a tray just like she does when I'm ill.'

'Are you sure?' said Dad.

'I can *do it*!' I insisted, just as Honeyblossom's wails became a notch louder.

'Well, all right!' said Dad, looking somewhat relieved. 'Just make sure you

don't spill anything when you're carrying
the tray upstairs.'

As he hurried out of the room,
I beamed at Mum.

'I'm going to look after you!'
I promised. 'And I'll do it so well that
you'll be *completely* better tomorrow, and
we can go on a picnic! But first . . .'

Before she could even reply, I raced
back to my room, took off my pyjamas,
and rummaged in my dressing-up box
for my nurse's uniform. Then I sped back
downstairs and in to see Mum.

'Ah, hello there, Nurse Isadora!' she said, smiling back at me. 'I think I have fairy flu; what do you prescribe?'

'Strawberries!' I said firmly. 'A whole bowl of them.'

'I think I need more rest first . . .' said Mum. 'But a bowl of strawberries in a little bit *would* be lovely.'

'I'll go and get them,' I said. 'But let me fluff up your pillows and straighten your duvet first.'

I spent a few minutes patting Mum's pillow and smoothing down her blanket.

'Do you want me to brush your hair for you?' I asked. 'So that it doesn't get tangled?'

'Er, no, that's OK,' said Mum weakly. 'I'll do it later.'

'Are you sure?' I asked, hurrying over to the dressing table and picking up Mum's fairy hairbrush. 'I can do it *really* gently.'

'I know,' said Mum. 'Thank you. But first I just need a little more sleep . . .'

'How about if I—?'

'Isadora!' came Dad's voice from next door. 'Are you getting the strawberries?

14

Let Mum rest!'

I dropped the hairbrush and scooted
out of the room.

'Back soon!' I called over my shoulder.

Chapter TWO

I flew out into the garden with Mum's gardening basket slung over my shoulder. Mum is really big on gardening (all fairies love nature) so she has a special vegetable patch where she grows all kinds of things! There are cucumbers, lettuces, strawberries, raspberries, and in the autumn, huge orange pumpkins! Next to the vegetable patch there are a couple of fruit trees covered in cherries and peaches. I knelt down and began picking some of the juicy red strawberries, popping them into the basket. They looked so delicious that I couldn't resist snacking on a few!

Some of them even twinkled faintly in the sunlight. Mum does like to use a sprinkling of magic and you can definitely taste the difference.

'There!' I said to Pink Rabbit once the basket was full. 'Mum will be pleased with all these!'

I walked back to the house and
into the kitchen where I washed the
strawberries and put them in a bowl.
Then I put the bowl on a tray.

'Hmm,' I said. 'It all looks a bit plain
to me.'

I wished that I could bring something
up for Mum that was a bit more special.
When I'm ill, Mum cuts my fruit into
stars or moons and makes me toast and a
smoothie to go with it. What could make
Mum's strawberries more interesting?

Sprinkles and whipped cream!

My mouth watered at the thought.
It would be nice to do something to cheer
Mum up, and she would be *so* surprised . . .

I went over to the fridge and pulled out a can of pink squirty whipped cream and hunted in the cake decorating drawer. Then I set to work covering the strawberries in a huge swirl of fluffy whipped cream and shaking rainbow sprinkles on top of it. I added a drizzle of chocolate sauce for good measure.

'Yum!' I said. 'This is sure to make Mum feel better!'

I looked at my swirly multicoloured creation and wondered what else I could add to create the most interesting and pretty tray that Mum had ever seen! I scavenged around the kitchen for more food, making buttered toast with sugared rose petals on top and asking our resident ghost Oscar to make the tea. He can use the kitchen appliances by himself because he's more than two hundred years old! I finished off by filling a vase with water and picking a get-well daisy from the garden. When I was finished the whole thing looked *beautiful*.

'Mum's going to be so pleased!' I said to Oscar and Pink Rabbit as I proudly and carefully carried the tray out of the kitchen and back up the stairs. Oscar floated along next to me, carrying the cup

of tea. The tray was very heavy, and the
vase almost toppled over, but eventually, I
made it to Mum and Dad's bedroom door
and gently nudged it open.

'Hi, Mum!' I said, cheerfully. 'I've brought you something to make you feel better!'

I put the tray down on her bedside table so that she could look at it properly. She didn't say anything for a moment.

'That's really . . . lovely, Isadora,' she said eventually. 'I love the pretty daisy. Err . . . where are the strawberries?'

'Under the whipped cream!' I said.

'They looked a bit boring on their own so I thought you might like the sprinkles and cream and chocolate sauce! And I've made you some toast, look! And a cup of tea. Well, Oscar made the tea.'

'I see,' said Mum, turning a little green. 'How thoughtful. Thank you, darling. I think I'll, er . . . eat it all in a bit?'

'OK!' I nodded. 'What would you like to do in the meantime? I know! I'll get your fairy magazines for you to read!'

Before Mum could reply I shot out of the room and back down the stairs, gathering up all Mum's magazines from their various places round the house.

'Here you are!' I cried, bursting back
into Mum and Dad's bedroom and dumping
the magazines down on the bed. 'Shall I sit
here and read them with you? Do you want
the light on? It's *very* dark in here. It must
be so boring being here on your own. I'm
sure you'll get better much more quickly
if you're not feeling lonely. We could do a
wordsearch together!'

Mum smiled in a strained sort of way.

'You're being very kind, Isadora,' she said. 'But I think I just need more sleep.'

'I wouldn't mind a nap too!' I said. 'Well, I'm actually quite awake, but I could *lie* next to you at least, or tell you a story. Give me a moment to think of one.'

I snuggled down with Mum under the covers just as Dad poked his head into the room. He had Honeyblossom on his hip and she was sucking on her bottle.

'Everything all right in here?' he asked. 'Isadora, what are you doing? Mum needs to rest. Come on out and find something to do.'

'But I'm *helping*.'

27

Dad's eyes flicked to the tray on the bedside table. He frowned.

'Why did you bring all that?' he asked. 'Where are the strawberries?'

'Under the whipped cream and rainbow sprinkles!' I replied, starting to feel a little exasperated.

'Right,' said Dad, his frown deepening. 'That's very creative, but fairy flu isn't cured with whipped cream and sprinkles. I'll wash the strawberries clean, Cordelia, and bring them back right away. Honeyblossom's happy so don't worry about a thing.'

I stared at Mum in shock, expecting her to tell Dad that sprinkles and cream were *exactly* what she fancied and that they would make her feel *better*, but she didn't say anything! She just smiled wearily. Had I got it so very wrong?

I was only trying to help!

'Come on out, Isadora,' said Dad. 'Let's leave Mum to sleep.'

I slid out of the bed, dragging my heels and feeling a bit silly.

Chapter THREE

'Why don't you play with Honeyblossom
while I make your breakfast?' suggested
Dad.

'All right,' I sighed.

As I did a bat-shaped jigsaw puzzle
with my baby sister, I tried to think of
other things I might be able to do to help
Mum feel better. I *so* wanted to look after

her really well, the way she always looks
after me. What could I *do*?

I was just helping Honeyblossom to
put the last piece into the puzzle when I
had a brilliant idea: *a bath*!

I love having a nice warm bath when I'm unwell. Mum always runs me one with lots of bubbles in it, so that must be how she likes it too!

Mum doesn't often use the bath inside the house, she prefers the garden pond—fairies love being close to nature!

But surely she wouldn't want to bathe in the pond while she was ill? A warm bubbly soak in the family bathroom would probably be good for her! I could sprinkle rose petals in it and put Dad's vampire candles around it!

It would be *so* relaxing.

After breakfast, I ran out of the kitchen and back up the stairs to the bathroom. Excitedly, I turned on the taps. Mum doesn't have any bubble bath in the pond (it would be bad for the fish, and she likes the plant smells and natural green water) but I was sure she'd want some indoors. I found some of Dad's in the cupboard under the sink. It was very red and smelled strongly of strawberry-scented freesias—although there didn't seem to be much of the mixture left. I turned the bottle upside down over the water.

Squeeze, squeeze, squeeeeeze!

'Hmm,' I said to Pink Rabbit when

there was no more mixture left in the bottle. 'The water isn't as bubbly as I'd like.'

Pink Rabbit pointed to my magic wand and wiggled his ears.

'I suppose I *could* do a spell,' I said, picking it up. 'I saw Mum doing bubble spells for Honeyblossom the other day. It looked easy!'

I waved my wand above the bathtub, envisioning more bubbles appearing on the water. Stars and glitter fizzled in the air.

POP! *Pop!* POP!

More bubbles began to appear, sparkling and glinting.

'Ooh!' I said, scooping up a massive handful and sniffing in the lovely flowery scent. Fairy magic can be a bit tricky for me sometimes as I am only *half* fairy so I felt really pleased with myself!

'That was a perfect idea, Pink Rabbit!'

I said, turning off the taps now and taking his paw. 'Let's go and fetch some rose petals!'

Pink Rabbit and I headed down the stairs and back out into the garden. Mum loves flowers and she has loads of roses!

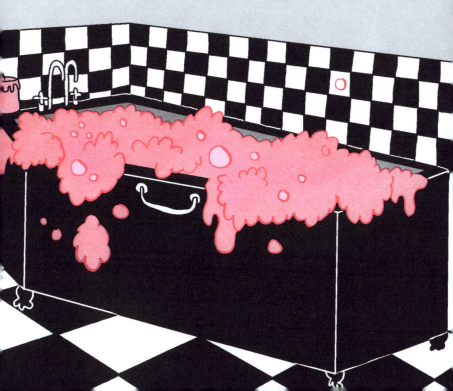

I found a bush that had lots of petals scattered beneath it and scooped them all up. They were so pink and velvety. I sprinkled them all into my basket like confetti. I couldn't wait to sprinkle them into the bubbly bath. It would be like making a magic potion!

'Right!' I said to Pink Rabbit. 'Back to the bathroom we go!'

We marched back into the house, feeling as though we were on a mission. Halfway up the stairs I could already smell the bath, and from across the landing I could see a few stray bubbles floating out of the bathroom door!

'My spell must have really done its work by now!' I said, feeling pleased.

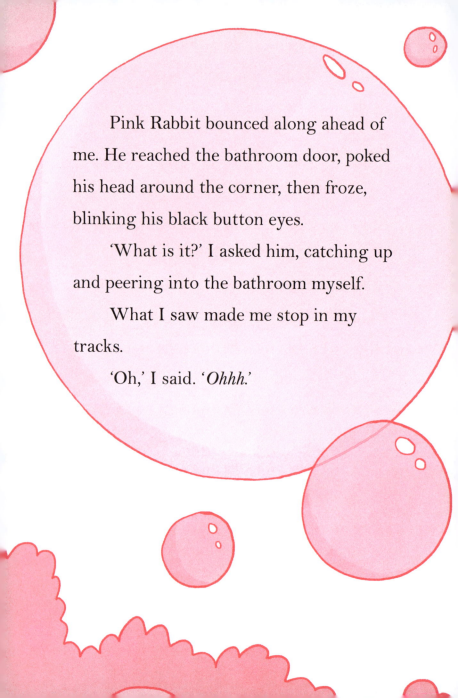

Pink Rabbit bounced along ahead of me. He reached the bathroom door, poked his head around the corner, then froze, blinking his black button eyes.

'What is it?' I asked him, catching up and peering into the bathroom myself.

What I saw made me stop in my tracks.

'Oh,' I said. '*Ohhh.*'

The bathroom was full to the *brim* with gleaming rainbow bubbles! There were so many that I couldn't even see the bath, or the sink, or the toilet. Stepping inside was like walking into a cloud! A few bubbles popped against me as I pushed through, but more replaced them just as fast. And then . . .

'WOAH!' I cried as my foot slipped ahead of me across the wet, sudsy floor, sending me flying up into the air and then—

'Ouch!'

I landed right on my bottom!

'Oh dear,' I groaned to Pink Rabbit, reaching for my wand. 'Maybe I was a bit too enthusiastic with the spell . . .'

I waved my wand again, envisioning a bathroom with *far fewer* bubbles. Stars and glitter sparkled through the air.

And then . . .

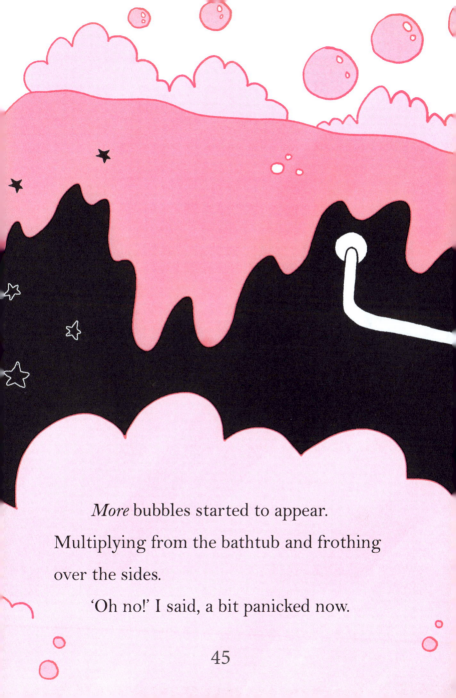

More bubbles started to appear.
Multiplying from the bathtub and frothing
over the sides.

'Oh no!' I said, a bit panicked now.

45

Dad wasn't going to be happy. He already had enough on his plate looking after Mum and Honeyblossom, and I'd told him I would be fine! But I couldn't *not* let him know about the bubbles. At this rate, they would probably get to him before I could, anyway!

Carefully, I crawled back across the slippery floor and back onto the landing, Pink Rabbit sliding along behind me grumpily. He does not like getting wet. We went downstairs and into the kitchen. Dad was standing by the sink, washing up with his sunglasses on, while Honeyblossom played with her fluffy toy bat by his feet.

'These pots and pans are so shiny,' he grumbled.

I sidled up to Dad.

'Err,' I began. 'Dad, I have a . . . *situation* in the, um . . . bathroom.'

Dad turned to look at me.

'You're all wet!' he said, lifting his sunglasses to see me better. 'And Pink Rabbit too! Why is there rainbow foam in your hair?'

I blushed a deep pink. Next to me, Pink Rabbit crossed his arms over his chest haughtily.

'I was just practising my fairy magic,' I said. 'You know, like Mum's always telling me to? But I think I made a mistake. I don't know how to fix it. I wanted to run a nice bath for Mum to help her feel better, but the bottle was nearly empty and I squeezed and squeezed and there weren't enough bubbles and . . .'

Dad sighed, putting down the pan he was holding and carefully stashing the scrubbing brush in its holder.

'All right,' he said, waving me ahead. 'Let's have a look . . .'

Chapter FOUR

'What in the name of batwings . . . ?' muttered Dad. He marched along to the bathroom, his black cape flapping behind him, as bubbles puffed out of the door in great clouds.

'Wait!' I called. 'It's really slip—!'

'ARGHHH!'

I hurried along the landing, swatting

away the bubbles.

'Dad! Are you all right?'

Dad was sitting on the bathroom floor, rubbing his hip with one hand, and waving his other hand about in the air to try and pop as many bubbles as possible.

He kept muttering lots of short, sharp words under his breath. But the more he popped the bubbles, the faster they appeared!

Dad gripped the rim of the bath and pulled himself to his knees. Then, through the popping of the bubbles, I heard him pull the plug out of the bath and the water start to drain away.

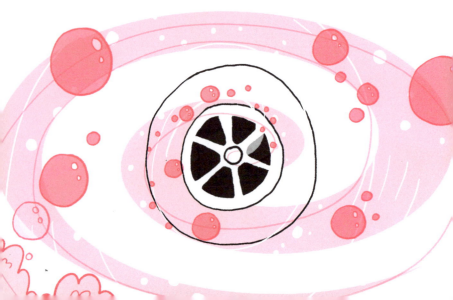

'Maybe that will help,' he said despairingly, crawling back across the floor. 'But I don't know how to fix fairy magic . . . Let's just close the door. I'm sure the magic will wear off soon, won't it, Isadora? Does fairy magic usually . . . stop?'

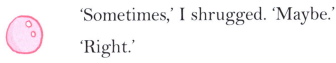

'Sometimes,' I shrugged. 'Maybe.'

'Right.'

'I'm sorry, Dad. I was trying to be helpful for Mum, and I've made a problem for you . . .'

'You're very sweet,' said Dad, closing the bathroom door firmly. 'But there's really not much you need to do for Mum. She just needs rest.'

'OK,' I said, in a small voice.

Dad put his hand on my shoulder.

'It's easy to get so carried away trying to make someone happy that you forget to listen to what they actually want,' he said. 'I once bought Mum a whole box of *delicious* vampire chocolates, filled with red juice for our wedding anniversary!'

'But Mum hates red juice!' I gasped.

'Exactly,' said Dad. 'I was so busy thinking about what I would like to receive as a gift, that I forgot that fairies don't like red juice.'

I giggled. Dad always has a way of making me feel better about a mistake.

54

'I wish I *could* do something helpful though,' I said.

Dad's face suddenly lit up.

'Actually,' he said. 'There is something you could do. Something very helpful!'

'Ooh, what?!' I asked. *Anything!'*

'You could tidy your room!' said Dad. 'Now that's a *wonderful* idea! Mum would be delighted, I'm sure!'

I felt my face fall. Maybe I hadn't really meant *'anything'*.

'But . . .' I began.

'No buts!' said Dad. 'You agreed! *Off you pop*!'

I trudged up to my turret bedroom, feeling utterly deflated. I really didn't see how tidying my room would help Mum— she wasn't recovering in *my* bed—but when I gazed around at my floor with all the clothes and toys strewn across it, I had to admit to myself that it could do with a clean.

I set to work picking things up and putting them away, but it was hard to stay focused, especially as it was so lovely and light and bright outside . . . The sun streamed through the window, and it felt like such a shame to be stuck indoors. Eventually, I stopped tidying and went over to the window, putting my chin on my hands as I stared down at the garden. I could see Mum's large greenhouse down near her vegetable patch, and I thought about how that was probably quite messy inside too—just like my bedroom! Mum is not the tidiest fairy around.

Then I had an idea.

Tidying my bedroom *would* be nice

for Mum but surely tidying *her greenhouse* would be even nicer! She would be so surprised and delighted to find it all spick and span once she was better. Plus, it would be a much more interesting thing to do than tidying my bedroom. I love poking about in all Mum's magical fairy things . . .

Feeling a bit more enthusiastic, I ran back down the stairs with Pink Rabbit hopping along behind me. I scooted past the kitchen where Dad was busy sweeping the floor, and out into the garden.

'I'm sure Dad won't mind me not tidying my room if I'm cleaning Mum's greenhouse,' I said to Pink Rabbit as we skipped down the garden path. 'It's still *tidying*, isn't it?'

Pink Rabbit didn't seem to agree outright, but he still came along, so I took that for approval as I pushed open the door of Mum's greenhouse with a creak.

Inside, it smelled strongly of soil and leaves and compost.

'*Mmm,*' I said, imitating Mum. 'It smells of *nature!*'

Pink Rabbit giggled. I could tell he was giggling because he squeezed his button eyes shut and put his paw over his mouth. Together we stepped into the greenhouse and closed the door behind us.

'It is a bit of a mess, isn't it?' I said, gazing around. There were piles of spilt soil everywhere, garden tools scattered across the floor, and packets of seeds piled haphazardly on the surfaces.

'Oh dear,' I said, suddenly feeling a little overwhelmed. 'Where to start?'

Pink Rabbit pointed at a pair of gloves.

'Oh yes, you're right!' I said, reaching for the gloves. 'Mum says to always wear gloves when gardening!'

I pulled the big, heavy gloves over my hands and halfway up my arms, then took a long-handled brush and began to sweep the floor. As I swept, I began to sing and dance, practising some of my ballet moves and twirling around the handle of the brush. Pink Rabbit followed me. He loves dancing too.

This was already so much more fun than tidying my room!

'Wheee!' I cried, spinning and swirling around before crashing into a rickety wooden table and knocking a bag of something off it.

'*Oops!*'

I stared down at the floor. The bag had split open and some of Mum's special fairy-dust soil twinkled prettily up at me.

The fairy-dust soil that she told me never to touch with bare skin. The soil that makes her plants grow *extra* big, *extra* fast.

I felt my heart start to pitter-patter *ever so slightly.*

'It's OK,' I said to Pink Rabbit, who was now staring accusingly at me with his button eyes. 'We can clear this up. I'm wearing gloves so I won't touch it. But maybe no more dancing . . .'

I got a dustpan and brush and set to work, carefully clearing the explosion of sparkly soil back into the bag.

'There!' I said. Although there was still a bit of a glittery sheen on the floor and on the knees of my trousers where I had accidentally knelt in it. I tried to brush it off with my gloved hands, but it only sent shimmery clouds puffing into the air which I tried not to breathe in. I stepped back and took the gloves off, letting them drop to the floor, then I backed out of the greenhouse.

On my way back through the garden, I wondered if maybe it would have been safer *not* to tidy it after all . . .

'Isadora?' said Dad, spotting me through the kitchen window and poking his head out. 'What are you up to? I

thought you were tidying your bedroom?'

'I'm just on my way upstairs to carry
on with it!' I replied.

'Marvellous!' said Dad. 'On your way
up, please could you give this to Mum?'

He held out a glass of fizzy water and
I took it.

'Of course!' I said, delighted.

Chapter FIVE

Carefully I carried the glass of water up the stairs.

'Mum?' I whispered as I pushed open the bedroom door.

Mum pushed herself up on her pillows looking a little more refreshed than earlier.

'Oh, hello there, Nurse Isadora,' she

smiled, trying to flatten her hair. 'What have you been up to?'

'Uh,' I said, blushing, '*just* tidying.'

'Lovely,' said Mum, taking the glass from me and having a sip. Then she frowned.

'Your clothes look ever so slightly sparkly,' she said. 'And a bit dirty? Especially your trousers . . .'

Before I could step back, she had reached out and brushed some of the glittery soil off my nurse's outfit. I gulped, hoping that there wasn't enough of it to have any effect. I didn't think now was the right time to tell Mum that I had spilt some of her magic soil. Not when she was ill!

Mum ran her fingers through her hair as she melted back down into her pillows.

'Don't want to get tangles,' she murmured sleepily. 'Oh, it's *so* lovely to

see you, my darling. Thank you for . . . the
water. But I think I need . . . to sleep more
now.'

I sat on the edge of the bed, keeping
an eye on Mum for a few minutes while
she slept, checking that the fairy-dust soil
wasn't doing anything weird. Everything
looked the same. There probably hadn't
been enough of it.

I tiptoed out of the room and gingerly shut the door. Out on the landing, I took off all the sparkling clothes, throwing them in a heap near the bathroom. Bubbles were still foaming out under the door, so I didn't dare go in for the laundry basket yet.

I ran up to my bedroom and searched the wardrobe for something that wasn't covered in magic soil. I pulled on a dress and a new pair of stripy tights (I have seven pairs—one for each day of the week!) and then looked around the chaos of my bedroom again, sighing despondently. It probably was time to get on with tidying . . .

★ ★ ★

I was just rearranging the furniture in my doll's house when I heard a worried shout from downstairs. My pointed ears pricked up. *What was going on?* Leaping up, I ran out of my room and down the stairs. What I saw made me stop in my tracks.

Honeyblossom!

She was sitting on the landing.

And she was *huge!*

Almost as big as Dad!

She was busy trying to pull my
trousers onto her head while Dad watched
in horror. Her skin was all covered in
glittery soil smudges.

'Oh no!' I gasped.

'What's happened?!' cried Dad, hopping up and down with panic and pulling at his hair so that it stood up in all directions. He looked like a frazzled scarecrow, with dark, sleepless rings under his eyes.

'What do we do, Isadora?' he asked. 'Is this fairy magic? Babies don't usually just grow massive! *You* never did anything like this when you were a baby!'

'Er . . .' I said. 'Um...'

'Isadora?'

'Oh, Dad! I'm so sorry! This is all *my* fault! It was a mistake! I thought it would be nice to clean Mum's greenhouse for her but I spilt some of her fairy-dust soil and cleaned it up but it got on my clothes but I couldn't get to the laundry basket so I . . . I dropped them on the floor.'

Dad turned pale, his jaw hanging open.

'I told you to tidy your *room*,' he cried. 'Not Mum's greenhouse!'

'I know,' I replied, hanging my head. 'But I just wanted to do something nice for Mum while she was ill. I thought tidying her greenhouse *would* be something she'd like!'

'I understand,' said Dad, taking a few slow, deep breaths to calm himself down. 'But there are reasons I ask you to do certain things and not others! Thank you for being honest though. At least now we know what the problem is, we can try and fix it. *Somehow.*'

We both gazed worriedly at my giant baby sister. She didn't seem to be bothered by her size—in fact, she seemed to be quite enjoying herself!

'Oh, I have *no idea* how to fix this!' Dad burst out. 'I've never understood fairy magic!'

'I have an idea!' I said. 'Let's ask Uncle Alvin and Aunt Seraphina!

They'll know what to do! They're always experimenting with lotions and potions for their beauty products. They're sure to know *everything* about fairy dust.'

'No, we *don't* need Uncle Alvin,' said Dad firmly. 'I don't want him thinking we can't look after things while his sister is poorly.'

We both stared at Honeyblossom.

Honeyblossom stared back.

'Let's call Uncle Alvin,' said Dad.

Chapter SIX

Dad hurried off to get the crystal ball
while I marvelled at my little sister now
being my BIG sister.

'I think you'd better put my trousers
down, Honeyblossom,' I told her. 'You
don't want to grow even bigger.'

But Honeyblossom just stared at
me and started trying to put them in her

mouth. I went to grab them, then scurried
backwards. It would be no good for *me* to
get the magic soil on *my* skin too! I would
have to just let Honeyblossom play.

Then I remembered Mum touching
the dust, and my insides squiggled with
anxiety.

Quietly, I opened the door to Mum
and Dad's room. She was still asleep, at
her usual size! At first glance, everything
seemed to be normal and I breathed a
sigh of relief.

But as my eyes adjusted to the dark, I noticed her hair.

All of her hair.

It was trailing down her body, off the side of the bed and curling onto the floor. She looked like Rapunzel!

'Oh no!' I whispered, sneaking out of the room and closing the door again. Now we had more than just Honeyblossom to worry about.

Wait.

Where was Honeyblossom?!

My trousers were in the middle of the floor, but she was nowhere to be seen. How could a giant baby *hide*? I squinted at the trousers, just in case she had shrunk down into them somehow, but then I noticed some bubbles hovering in the air further along the landing.

The bathroom door was open!

Hurriedly, I ran to the bathroom. *Of course* she would be big enough to use the

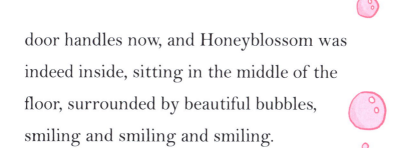

door handles now, and Honeyblossom was
indeed inside, sitting in the middle of the
floor, surrounded by beautiful bubbles,
smiling and smiling and smiling.

For a moment I forgot all about the mess I had caused. Honeyblossom *loves* bubbles! She was rolling around on the slippery floor and trying to pop them with her finger, getting all wet and giggling and . . .

Shrinking!

As the bubbles popped around her, Honeyblossom was slowly getting smaller.

'That must be the fix!' I gasped to Pink Rabbit. 'We just needed to wash off the fairy-dust soil!'

We didn't need Uncle Alvin after all!

'Dad!' I yelled, hurrying out of the bathroom. *'DAAAAD!'*

'Ssshh, Isadora!' said Dad, who was coming back up the stairs with the crystal ball in hand. Uncle Alvin's face was floating inside—and my cousin Mirabelle's too!

'*Isadora's causing mischief! Isadora's causing mischief!*' Mirabelle sang gleefully.

'I'm *not*!' I insisted, still too loud, then dropped to a grumble. 'I didn't *mean* to, anyway . . .'

But as I looked around at the bubbles, at Dad, at my clothes on the floor, I realized she might have a point. Was I turning into my naughty cousin Mirabelle?

'Sshh!' said Dad again. 'Listen, Isadora. Alvin knows the solution for shrinking Honeyblossom. There's a spell, but we'll need *you* to do it with your fairy wand because we can't ask Mum!'

'There's no need—' I began.

'Can't ask me *what*?' came Mum's voice through the bedroom door.

'Oh dear . . .' said Dad, sounding like he was losing hope.

He drew himself up, eased open the bedroom door, and we all peered in at Mum—even Uncle Alvin and Mirabelle from inside the crystal ball.

'Hello, Cordelia!' said Uncle Alvin. 'I'm sorry you're not well. Fairy flu, is it?'

'What's happened to your *hair*?!' squealed Mirabelle.

Mum gazed downwards.

'My *hair*!' she gasped. 'Am I still dreaming?'

'Unfortunately *not*, Aunt Cordelia!'

Dad turned slowly toward me, his frown returning.

'*ISADORA . . .*' he started.

'Where's Honeyblossom?' Mum said. 'Who's watching her?'

Honeyblossom!

For a moment we had all forgotten about my little sister.

'I'll . . . er, fetch her,' I said. 'She's safe in the bathroom.'

'*Safe?*' said Mum, looking even more confused now. 'In the *bathroom?*'

'*I'll* fetch her!' said Dad. 'Isadora won't be able to lift Honeyblossom in her . . . new state.'

'*What* state?' asked Mum, narrowing her eyes.

'No, I can!' I insisted. 'I *promise* I can!'

And before Dad could stop me, I ran off down the landing to the bathroom, scooped up my soaking-wet *little* baby sister, and carried her back to Dad.

'Whaa—?' gaped Dad. 'She's normal again!'

94

'*Normal?!*' said Mum, totally lost.
'When was she NOT?'

'Ah, you've found a spell already!' said
Uncle Alvin. 'Well done, Isadora!'

'It wasn't me really,' I said. 'It
was Honeyblossom. She went into the
bathroom to play with the bubbles and the
soapy water washed the soil off her!'

'Ah!' said Uncle Alvin sounding slightly embarrassed. 'I didn't think of that. Must note it down for future reference . . .'

'Soil?!' said Mum, weakly. 'Bubbles? I don't think I want to know!'

'There's no need for you to worry about any of it, Cordelia,' said Dad, wringing his hands. 'Everything's under control. I want you to feel *relaxed*. And I'm sorry about your hair. It's nothing serious. Theoretically, it should go back to normal as soon as you wash it. I'll run you a bath in my vampire ensuite, shall I? The family bathroom is er . . . out of use right now.'

'But it *will* be back in use tomorrow morning!' Uncle Alvin interjected, quickly. 'Bubble spells always wear off after a few hours.'

'Oh no, I don't want a bath!' said Mum, beaming. 'Especially not indoors. I *love* my new hair! I feel like a fairy princess!'

'Fairy-princess hair, huh?' said
Alvin. 'Now *that* would be a great beauty
product! So simply achieved, and easy to
wash out afterwards! I must conduct some
experiments. Goodbye, all!'

'Goodbye, Uncle Alvin!' I called.
'Goodbye, Mirabelle!'

'Bye, Isadora!' shouted Mirabelle. 'See
you soon!'

The crystal ball swirled with rosy-
pink fog and then went clear.

Chapter SEVEN

Mum swung her legs out of bed.

'I do feel better after that nap,' she said, stretching. 'Certainly well enough to come downstairs. I'll have a cup of nectar tea in the sitting room and watch Honeyblossom for a bit.'

'Oh no!' said Dad. 'You stay in bed and rest, Cordelia. I promise you, everything's under control!'

'I'm sure it is,' said Mum. 'But you look exhausted, Bartholomew, and it's getting boring being in bed. Have a sleep!'

'*Really?*' said Dad, looking longingly at the bed.

'Yes!' smiled Mum. 'And you can't catch fairy flu anyway, so you're safe.'

She took Honeyblossom from Dad and headed out of the bedroom, her long pink hair trailing behind her. She *did* look like a princess. I found myself feeling quite jealous!

'Just one last job before I can go to bed,' said Dad, going to look at my pile of clothes on the landing. 'We must get your

things in the washing machine, Isadora. We can't have any more of that soil anywhere. I'll fetch some tongs.'

'Wait!' I said. 'Let me do it. You go and rest.'

'Are you sure you can do it without getting any of the magic on you?' asked Dad.

I nodded, feeling a tiny spark of Mirabelle mischief flicker inside me.

'I definitely *can*,' I replied—but that didn't mean I *would*.

Dad gave a nervous nod, then a more confident one, before disappearing into the bedroom and closing the door.

I picked up my pile of clothes and

hurried downstairs with them as fast as possible, shoving them straight into the washing machine, then I ran my now sparkly fingers all the way through my hair!

Ten minutes later, I walked into the
sitting room with a tray of tea and fruit
for me, Mum, and Honeyblossom (Oscar
had helped make the tea!). As I walked,
I could feel my long, looong hair trailing
across the floor.

'Your mum's going to notice!' warned
Oscar.

'I *know*!' I giggled. 'But somehow
I don't think she'll mind.'

Mum looked up from where she
was sitting on the sofa with a happy
Honeyblossom on her lap. She was
conjuring bubbles from her wand
and Honeyblossom was trying to
pop them by clapping her hands.

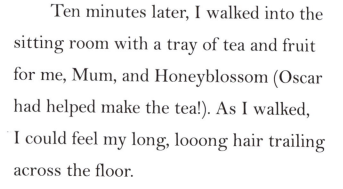

'I've brought you some tea and fruit,'
I said.

'Lovely,' smiled Mum,
looking up. 'Nice plain fruit
is just what I fancy today!'

Then she noticed
my hair.

'Isadora! Did you—?'

'Maybe.'

'Hmm. Did you wash your hands after?'

I nodded, unsure if it really had been a good idea.

'Well then . . .' She broke into a big, beaming smile. 'You're a fairy princess too now! How fun! Get up here.'

I put the tray down on the coffee table and jumped onto the sofa next to her, snuggling up.

'I know we can't have a picnic today,' I said, 'but I'm glad we can be fairy princesses together instead. *Quiet* fairy princesses, who do lots of resting. And if you do drop off to sleep, I'll practise my wand magic very softly and make us a couple of crowns. I've got some gold paper somewhere . . .'

'I could really do with a sparkly crown to cheer me up today!' said Mum. 'That sounds just *perfect*. Being fairy princesses is a much better idea than having an *indoor bubble bath!*'

Turn the page
for an
Isadorable
quiz!

What kind of caregiver are you?

Take the quiz to find out!

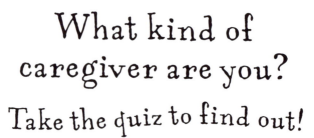

When someone you care about is feeling unwell, what's the first thing you do?

A. Make them a get-well card and cheer

them up with your artwork.

B. Offer to keep them company.

C. Bring them their favourite food

to make them feel better.

Your friend has a small cut on their finger. What do you do to help?

A. Find some colourful plasters and decorate

them for a magical touch.

B. Gently clean the wound

and give them a comforting hug.

C. Try to distract them so they

stop thinking about it.

How do you like to spend time with someone who needs your care?

A. Invent games to keep them entertained.

B. Listen to their stories and tell some of your own.

C. Fetch things that they need and do tasks that they need help with.

Mostly As
You're creatively caring, just like Isadora!
You bring joy and imagination to those in need.

Mostly Bs
You're a compassionate friend, like Isadora's mum!
You're gentle and caring, and your calm presence makes others feel better.

Mostly Cs
You're a practical problem-solver, the same as Isadora's dad! Anything that someone needs, you're there to sort it out.

Answers

MIRABELLE

Meet Isadora's naughty cousin,
Mirabelle Starspell, in her very own stories.

Get ready to meet Isadora's mermaid friend, Emerald!

From the world of ISADORA MOON

EMERALD
and the Ocean Parade

Plus fantastic activities!

The most rebellious princess under the sea

Harriet Muncaster

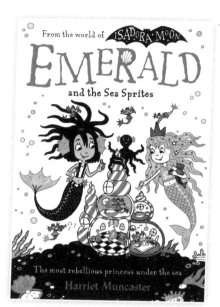

From the world of ISADORA MOON
EMERALD
and the Sea Sprites
The most rebellious princess under the sea
Harriet Muncaster

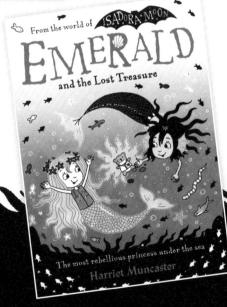

From the world of ISADORA MOON
EMERALD
and the Lost Treasure
The most rebellious princess under the sea
Harriet Muncaster

To visit Harriet Muncaster's website, go to
harrietmuncaster.co.uk

Harriet Muncaster

Harriet Muncaster, that's me! I'm the
creator of three young fiction series,
Isadora Moon, Mirabelle, and Emerald,
as well as the Victoria Stitch series for
older readers. I love anything teeny tiny,
anything starry, and everything glittery.

Love Isadora Moon?
Why not try these too . . .

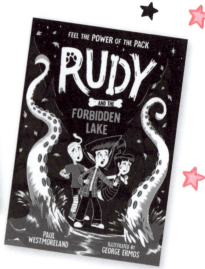